Courtney's BIRTHDAY PARTY

Inquiries should be addressed to

JUST US BOOKS, INC.
356 Glenwood Ave., East Orange, NJ 07017

Printed in Canada. First Edition
10 9 8 7 6 5 4 3 2 1
Library of Congress Cataloging in Publication Data is available.
ISBN: 0-940975-83-1

NOV 8 2001

it 99

AGL7057-1

CL

Seven, Seven, Seven
Will be just like heaven
In six days I'll be seven
In SIX days I'll be seven!

Courtney was going to be seven on Saturday, and it was all she could think about.

"I can't wait to tell Diana about my birthday party!" Courtney said as the school bus pulled up.

Courtney Crowley and Diana Davis were best friends. They lived in the same town, went to the same school, and were in the same class—where they sat in the same row. And they liked the same things: dinosaurs, jacks, and sunflower seeds—lots of sunflower seeds.

They were the same in almost every way. In just six days they'd even be the same age.

Courtney jumped onto the bus, ran to Diana, and sang a song she had made up.

Seven, Seven, Seven
Will be just like heaven
In six days I'll be seven
In SIX days I'll be seven!

"Oh, so you're finally gonna be seven, huh?" teased Diana.

"And I'm gonna have the best birthday party ever," said Courtney.

Without even taking a breath she added, "Mommy's getting every color balloon and five kinds of ice cream and a big strawberry cake and pizza and a Clown and dinosaur stickers for the party bags and all the sunflower seeds we can eat. All my family's coming and Mommy said I can invite the whole class — I'm bringing the invitations Wednesday."

As soon as Diana got home from school
she told her mother about Courtney's party.

"Please say I can go, Mommy, please."

"You've been invited?" Mrs. Davis asked.

"Courtney said the whole class can come —
plus, I'm her best friend."

"Oh, that's nice, honey," said Mrs. Davis,
"let me see the invitation."

"Courtney's bringing the invitations to school
on Wednesday," said Diana.

"Hmmm," was all Mrs. Davis said. She seemed
a little worried.

Mrs. Davis had gotten that same look on her
face when she asked Diana why Courtney never
played at their house.

"Oh, she wants to," Diana explained, "but her
mom's just been too busy to bring her."

Diana saw that look again when her mother
asked why Courtney never invited Diana to
her house.

"Oh, she has, Mommy," replied Diana.
"Courtney's mother always says it's not a good
time to have company."

"So can I go to the party?" Diana asked eagerly.

"We'll see," said Mrs. Davis, still looking a
little worried.

Grownups act so strange sometimes, thought
Diana. She dashed to her room. All she could
think about was the birthday party.

"I hope I have enough money to get Courtney a great present," she said to herself.

Diana counted the coins from her money pouch three times, and each time there was only $1.25—not enough.

Then she got an idea. "I can earn some money." Sure enough, she did.

Mr. Jones paid her a dollar to walk his dog, little Jitney.

Mrs. Washington paid her a dollar to go to the store.

Her mom gave her a few jobs to do around their house.

By Tuesday afternoon Diana had enough money to buy Courtney a pack of scrunchies for her hair plus a rainbow necklace.

"Courtney's gonna love these," Diana smiled.

Diana had as much fun wrapping the presents
as she did picking them out.

Seven, Seven, Seven
Will be just like heaven
In five days she'll be seven
In FIVE days she'll be seven!

Courtney said nothing. She just looked sad.

Wow, thought Diana, *something bad must have happened at home.*

Then Diana peeked into the shopping bag. The brightly colored envelopes made her smile.

"You can't fool me," Diana giggled. She reached into the bag and scooped out the envelopes. "I'll take mine now, okay?"

She read each name: "Melissa, Stephen, Janine, Nicholas, Judd, Lauren, Brandon, Theresa, Ryan, Howard, Gabriel . . ."

"Where's mine?" Diana frowned. Then she brightened. *Courtney must be trying to play a trick on me.*

"I don't have one for you," said Courtney, trying not to cry.

"I can't come to the party?" asked Diana. "Come on, stop fooling around."

Courtney lowered her head and wished she could disappear.

Now Diana's eyes were filling with tears. "But I got you a present and everything, plus you said everybody was invited…" Diana's voice trailed off into a whisper. "I thought you were my friend, my best friend."

"I am," Courtney said in a small, tearful voice.

Courtney took the invitations from Diana, threw them into the shopping bag and hurried toward an empty seat in the back of the bus. She quickly wiped away the big tears before they could roll down her cheeks.

When Diana sat back down, she turned to the window, wiping the tears from her eyes before the other children could see them.

When they finally got to school, Diana and Courtney left the bus alone.

Thursday and Friday were terrible for the two friends.

Courtney begged, "Mommy, please make an invitation for Diana."

"That's not a good idea, Courtney," Mrs. Crowley said. "One day you'll understand."

Courtney thought, *It's you who doesn't understand that Diana is my best friend. Don't you know that Diana's feelings were hurt because she wasn't invited? I'll never understand!*

Diana begged, "Please Mommy, please, call Mrs. Crowley and ask if I can come to the party."

"That's not a good idea, honey," Mrs. Davis said. "I know you're disappointed, but try not to let it ruin your whole weekend."

On Saturday Mrs. Davis had a surprise for Diana. Of course Diana thought it was an invitation to Courtney's birthday party. But it wasn't.

The surprise was a whole day at the mall—going to Diana's favorite stores, having double scoops at the ice cream shop, and seeing any movie Diana chose.

"I don't want to go to the mall," Diana said. *How can Mommy think the mall is better than Courtney's birthday party?* she thought.

Diana stared out the window in the direction of Courtney's house. Her gift for Courtney still sat neatly wrapped on the dresser. The outfit she'd picked out for the party still hung on the closet door.

There was a big sign outside Courtney's house that read "Happy Birthday Courtney!" And seven balloons were near the front door.

The cake was ready. Five kinds of ice cream were in the freezer. The pizza was on the way. The games were laid out. The party bags were filled. Everything was set. Most of the guests were there.

Courtney was dressed for the party, but she looked so sad. She sat at the window and wondered what Diana was doing.

"Courtney, your friends are waiting for you," Mrs. Crowley said. "It's your birthday!"

Courtney didn't say a word. She was thinking. *I won't get to sing the last and best part of my birthday song with Diana.*

> *Seven, Seven, Seven*
> *Will be just like heaven*
> *Seven, Seven, Seven*
> *Today we BOTH are...*

Suddenly, tears streamed down Courtney's cheeks.

Mrs. Crowley had never seen her daughter cry like that.

"Don't cry, Courtney" she said. "I'll see what I can do!"

R-i-n-g-g-g-g-g-g!

Mrs. Davis answered the phone. "Hello."

"Hello, this is Mrs. Crowley, Courtney's mom. Is this Mrs. Davis?"

"Yes, it is."

"It seems I made a mistake with the invitations for Courtney's birthday party. What I mean is, uh, well, that Diana should have been invited. Courtney is very unhappy. I don't think she'll have a good party if Diana's not here. I didn't realize they were best of friends."

"I did," answered Mrs. Davis.

"I know it's short notice, but can Diana come to the party?" Mrs. Crowley asked.

"Well, I don't know, Mrs. Crowley…Diana and I have plans, but let me ask Diana."

"Yes! Yes! Yes! Yes!" Diana shouted before her mother could say another word.

"I can pick her up," Mrs. Crowley offered.

"That won't be necessary," Mrs. Davis said. "I'll bring her."

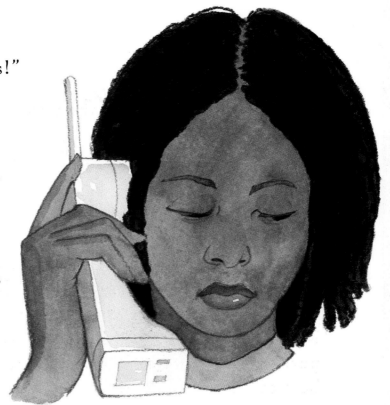

Diana rushed to her room. In a flash, she was at the front door—dressed in her party outfit and holding Courtney's birthday present in her hand.

"Before we go, Diana, we should have a little talk," her mother said. Diana noticed that worried look on her mother's face again.

"Now Courtney is your best friend, but Courtney's parents and your daddy and I don't know each other," Mrs. Davis explained. "In fact, even though we live in the same neighborhood, we probably would never get to know each other if it weren't for you girls."

"You see, some people only want to be with people who look like them. At work, or at school, it's difficult to avoid people who are different. But at a family celebration in their own homes, people can invite whomever they want."

"I think I know what you mean, Mommy, but Courtney's not like that. Courtney and I know that we are different on the outside, but we're the same on the inside," said Diana.

꿍

When Mrs. Davis's car came to a stop in front of Courtney's house, Diana jumped out and ran up the walkway.

Courtney ran to meet her and the two girls hugged so hard they almost fell to the ground.

Mrs. Davis smiled.

Mrs. Crowley smiled, too.

"It wouldn't have been a birthday party without my best friend," Courtney said to Diana.

Diana gave Courtney her present and the two friends skipped into the house. Their mothers followed them as the girls sang—

Seven, Seven, Seven
Just like heaven
Seven, Seven, Seven
Today we BOTH are seven!

COURTNEY'S BIRTHDAY PARTY

About the Author and the Illustrator

Dr. Loretta Long is an actress and educator, who has entertained children for over thirty years in her television role as "Susan" on Sesame Street. In addition to her work in entertainment, Dr. Long conducts diversity workshops for parents, librarians and educators. She earned a doctorate in education from the University of Massachussetts. This is her first picture book. She lives in West New York, NJ.

Ron Garnett is an accomplished illustrator and graphic designer who has illustrated several children's books including *Great Black Heroes: Five Notable Inventors* (Scholastic). This is his first picture book published by Just Us Books. Ron lives in Kansas City, MO.